P9-DFB-541

Gg Hh Ii Jj Kk Ll Mm

Uu Vv Ww Xx Yy Zz

Dear Parent,

The My First Steps to Reading® *series is based on a teaching activity that helps children learn to recognize letters and their sounds. The use of predictable language patterns and repetition of familiar words will also help your child build a basic sight vocabulary. Your child will enjoy watching the characters in the books place imaginative objects in "letter boxes." You and your child can even create and fill your own letter box, using stuffed animals, cut-out pictures, or other objects beginning with the same letter. The things you can do together are limited only by your imagination. Learning letters will be fun—the first important step on the road to reading.*

The Editors

© 2001 The Child's World, Inc.
All Rights Reserved. Published by Scholastic Inc., 90 Old Sherman Turnpike, Danbury, Connecticut 06810,
by arrangement with The Child's World, Inc.
Scholastic offers a varied selection of children's book racks and tote bags. For details about ordering, please write to:
Scholastic At Home, 90 Old Sherman Turnpike, Danbury, CT 06810, Attention: Premium Department

Originally published as *My "k" Sound Box* by The Child's World, Inc.

My First Steps to Reading is a registered trademark of Grolier Publishing Co. Inc.
SCHOLASTIC and associated logos are trademarks and/or registered trademarks of Scholastic Inc.

No part of this publication may be reproduced, or stored in a retrieval system, or transmitted in any form or by any means,
electronic, mechanical, photocopying, recording, or otherwise, without written permission of the publisher.
For information regarding permission, write to The Child's World, Inc., P.O. Box 326, Chanhassen, MN 55317.
ISBN 0-7172-6510-2

Printed in the U.S.A.

My "k" Book

written by Jane Belk Moncure

illustrated by Colin King

Little 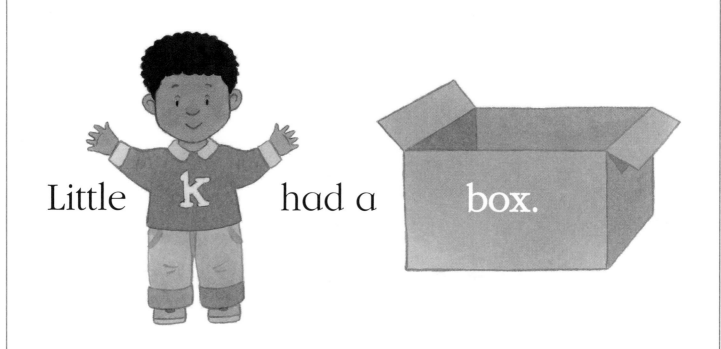 had a box.

"I will find things that begin
with my 'k' sound," he said.

"I will put them into my sound  box."

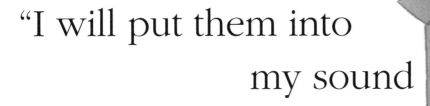

"But first, I will be a king."

So he dressed up as a king.

Then Little  went for a walk.

He found a koala.

Did he put the koala into his box?
He did.

Next, Little K found

some kingfishers.

Did he put the kingfishers
into his box? He did.

Then Little  found a kitty.

"Kitty, kitty," he called.

Lots and lots of kittens came . . .

from everywhere!

Little  tried to put the kittens into the box. But the kingfishers did not like it!

Do you know why?

What could Little K do?

He found a . . .

The kangaroo had a big pocket.

Little  put all the kittens
                              into the pocket.

"A king can do anything!"

said Little .

So he played the kettledrum.
Then he put it into his box.

Next, he looked through a kaleidoscope.

Here is what he saw.

He put the kaleidoscope into his box, too.

Then Little found kites,

lots and lots of kites.

"I will fly a kite," he said.

But the wind blew the kite away.
The kingfishers flew after the kite.

The kittens kicked the kangaroo.

The kangaroo sneezed, "Kerchoo!"
and blew . . .

everything into a . . .

kindergarten classroom.

My, what fun the children had!

kites

kingfishers

kitten

kettledrum

kingfisher

kangaroo

kitten

koala

kittens

kitten

Can you read these words with Little  ?

kiss

ketchup

kettle

key

kitchen

kid

kid

kayak

Aa Bb Cc Dd Ee Ff

Nn Oo Pp Qq Rr Ss Tt

My First Steps to READING®